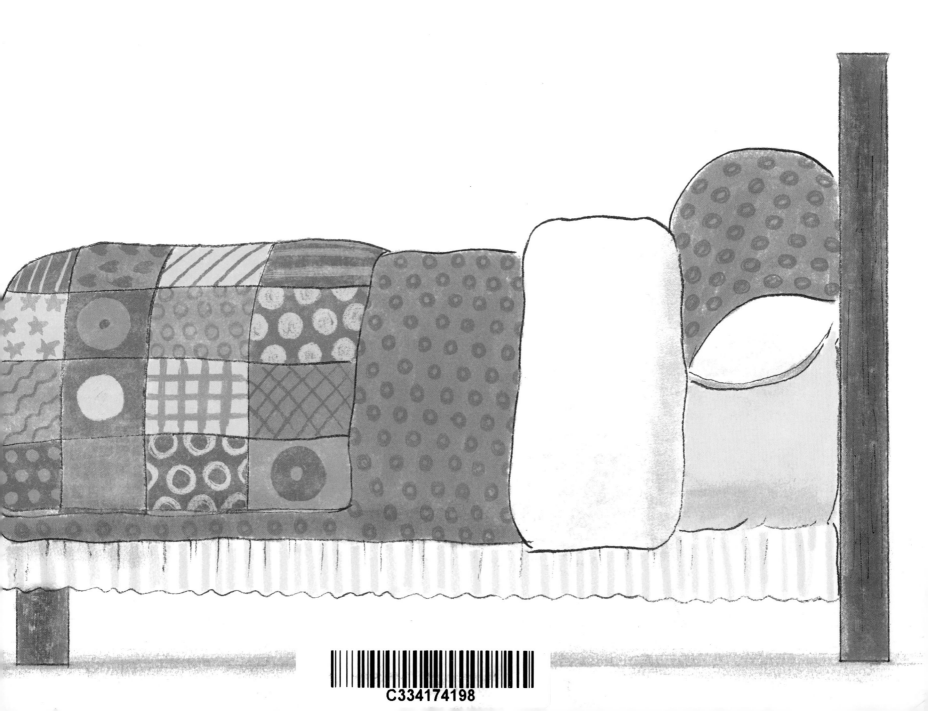

Goodnight, Rolo. Sleep well

First published in Great Britain in 2018 by Hodder and Stoughton

Hodder Children's Books
An imprint of Hachette Children's Group
Part of Hodder and Stoughton
Carmelite House
50 Victoria Embankment
London EC4Y 0DZ

ISBN 978 1 444 92788 7

1 3 5 7 9 10 8 6 4 2

Printed in China

An Hachette UK Company
www.hachette.co.uk

Hodder
Children's
Books

MIX
Paper from
responsible sources
FSC
www.fsc.org
FSC® C104740

Goodnight, Mr Panda

Steve Antony

I am going to bed.
Goodnight, Mr Panda.

You've forgotten to brush your teeth.

I'll brush them
twice in the
morning.

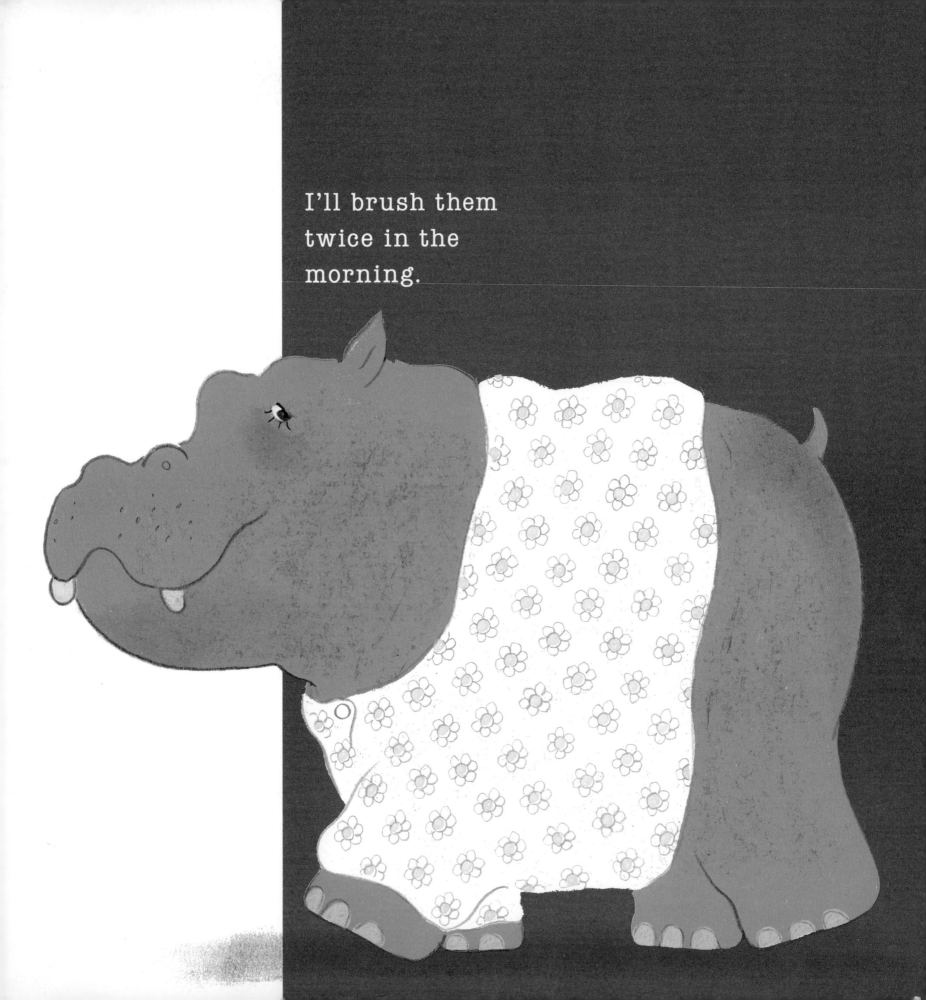

My mouth is minty fresh!

Goodnight, Hippo.

I'm going to bed, too.
Goodnight, Mr Panda.

You've forgotten to have a bath.

But I had
a bath
last year.

I'm
as
fresh
as
a
daisy!

Goodnight, Skunk.

We are going to bed. Goodnight, Mr Panda.

You've forgotten
your pyjamas.

Sheep don't
wear pyjamas.

Goodnight, Sheep.

But lemurs do!

You should go to bed, Sloth.

I'm too tired to move.

Mr Panda, are you
going to bed?

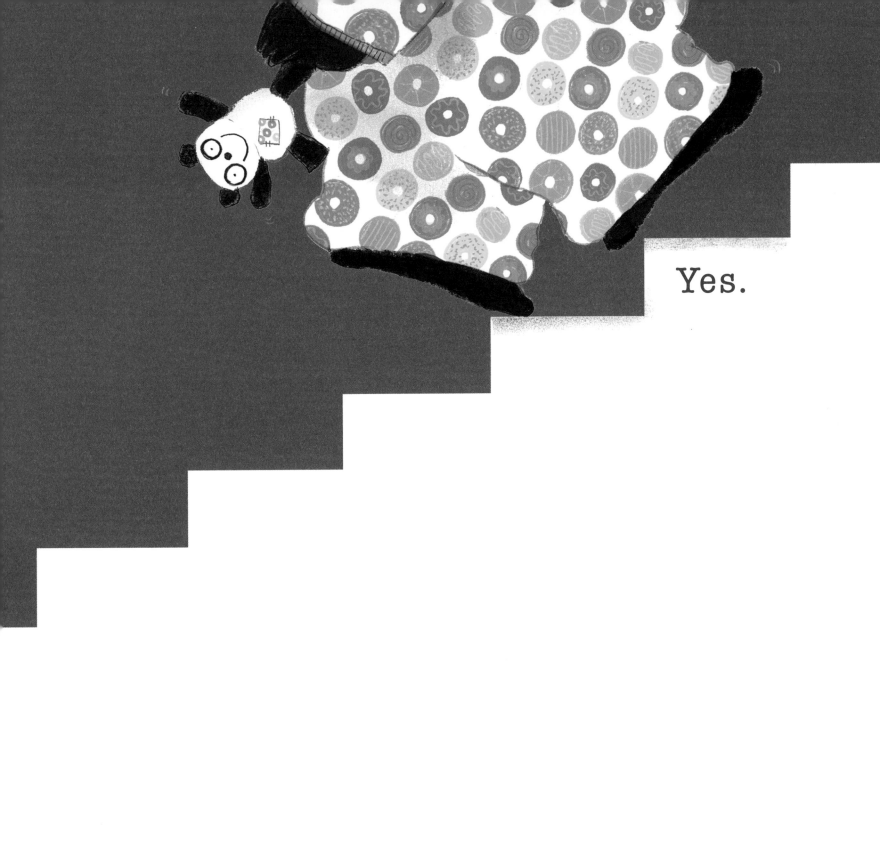

Yes.

Haven't you
forgotten
something?

Goodnight, Lemur.

Goodnight, Mr Panda.

But Mr Panda...

...that's my bed!